ALPHA

The story of Tanner Ronin

An Elite Series Novella

Original story by

John Mark Tucker

Cover Art by Molly Phipps
wegotyoucoveredbookdesign.com

Editing by Christine LePorte
cleporte@gmail.com

Copyright © 2019 John Mark Tucker
All rights reserved.
johnmarktucker.com

ISBN: 9781793320186
Independently published

For everyone's father.

Here or gone. Far or near.

Table of Contents

Prologue 6
1 15
2 17
3 25
4 28
5 31
6 34
7 39
8 45
9 47
10 52
11 57
12 64
13 70
14 73
15 75
16 78
17 83
18 85
19 88
20 90

21	98
22	105
23	111

Prologue

Fourteen years before Elite: One

When I was ten, I remember sitting on one of the swings that was in our skyscraper's indoor park. Looking up, I was surrounded on four sides by windows and balconies that stretched two hundred stories above me. My mom and dad were up there, all the way at the top. They were having another party. Another gathering of my father's mindless, groveling friends. He had returned again from a successful mission. And as had happened every time in the past, our home was soon flooded with Gamas eager to hear my father tell tales of ripping Terrans to pieces. Slicing them in half. Shooting them in the head. Crushing and dominating them. I finally had enough when he described how he squeezed a Terran's neck so hard blood shot out of the soldier's eyes and nose.

So I found my FollowMe ball and went down to the park. I swayed a little on the swing, tossing my ball a few feet away and catching it when it obediently returned to my hands. There were other children in the park around my age, but they just stared and pointed. Whispering unknown things about me and my father. They knew who I was and they knew who he was. Elite Alpha Vladion Ronin. Our people's mightiest soldier. A symbol of our military strength personified into one figure. They knew I was already in training. Twenty hours a week of hand-to-hand, blade, and rifle combat. When he wasn't on a mission, my father would come every day and pick me up. The other students in the classroom would watch silently as I gathered my books and backpack and walked out of the room as he held the door open for me. Off to more training.

"Did the party get a little loud for you, boy?" My father's voice startled me and I looked to see him on the next swing over.

"Oh, yeah. A little. Sorry." I flushed red in embarrassment.

He snuck up on me. He's going to say something about that...

"That was a little too easy for me to surprise you like that, Tanner. You'll have to do better, you know. You have to be more aware of your surroundings."

"I know, Father," slumping in my swing.

"Do you not like my stories anymore? Everyone else loves my stories," he said, looking at me with stern eyes. I shrugged, unsure what to say other than it couldn't be the truth.

"Your father won another battle for our people, Tanner. Doesn't that make you proud of me? Doesn't that make you happy to be my boy?"

I didn't know. It all seemed so very harsh.

In a flash of bravery...no...stupidity, I actually answered with what I wanted to say.

"Have...have you ever asked *why* you have to go and kill all those Terrans?"

My father's expression changed three distinct times in as many seconds. First, surprise, followed by anger and finally settling into disappointment. The worst of the three. He took a deep breath and looked down at me with thin lips.

"The *why* is not important, Tanner. *Why* doesn't matter. We are Gama. They are Terran. We are right and they are wrong. It's that simple. And with every Gama victory that I lead, the Ronin name becomes more beloved by our people and the Elite Alpha crown becomes more feared by the Terrans. THAT is what is important, son. You will understand, someday. You will be like me in ten or so years. Whether it is standing on a battlefield or walking through the streets of Palertine, people will look at you like you are a god. And that's exactly what you will be, Tanner. A god among the people of this world."

His eyes had turned wild, like they did when he told of his battles, and I said the thing I should have said in the first place.

"Yes, Father. I understand."

"That's my boy, Tanner. Come upstairs when you're done playing. Your mother made a cake for me." He smiled and gave a fatherly pat on my head as he left.

Yes. I remember that moment so vividly. That was the real moment when I began my journey to become an Elite.

Two years before Elite: One

I lay on my back at the top of a ridge, staring at the setting star in front of me. It was similar to Palertine's star and cast a gorgeous orange hue to the sky above and the ground below. My ears were filled with radio chatter from the battle winding down just on the other side of this ridge I was on. We were there to take over a small Terran military outpost in the middle of god-knows nowhere important.

Why?

My father was strangely right with his *whys are not important* speech. He wasn't alone with that thought process. Turns out about everyone in charge thinks the same way.

Just do.

Don't think.

Pull the trigger first, ask who it was and what they wanted second. And then take that exact same mentality and put it in charge of the Terran military and you end up with a complete God damned cluster fuck of madness. In the end, what got quietly mumbled, when no one important was listening, was that battles are good for the economy. There are twenty billion

Gamas in the galaxy. Ten billion were involved in the Gama Military Collective in one way or another. So, losing fifty or sixty soldiers every day was no biggie. As long as we kept the money turning and churning, everything was copacetic.

I hadn't really put a whole lot of energy into today's battle. We started about four hours ago with three hundred Gama grunts on the ground and an estimated hundred fifty Terran army brats protecting their little fort. From the chatter, it sounds like we have lost around a hundred and they have lost the same. But those last fifty remaining Terrans are really dug in and causing all sorts of hell with the Gama soldiers. Right or wrong, two hours ago I just switched off my commset and took a nice nap.

Now, though, I needed to get to work. I mean, I was Elite Alpha for Christ's sake.

"Command, do we have any frequencies that the Terrans are communicating on?" trying not to yawn.

"Standby, Elite," Command quipped formally in my ear. I got up and stretched, my Elite suit creaking and squeaking as it warmed up to its wearer.

Command spoke.

"We have one channel. It's not been used for anything important, though. They've kept that all scrambled."

"Roger, Command, patch me into that channel we have. I'm going to radio a message directly to them. Also patch me into the main Gama commlink as well. I want everyone to hear this," still stretching and doing some squats as I spoke. There was a click in my ear.

"Roger, Elite. Your mic is hot."

I walked the ten or so feet up my side of the ridge to the very top. The setting sun was now behind me, casting a forty-foot-long shadow down the ridge's side. Below were a mess of smoking vehicles, the Terran base, and a bunch of Gama soldiers that looked like ants running around. Blind ants.

Blind leading the blind...

"Attention all Terran soldiers. This is Elite Alpha of the Gama Military Collective. I am on the lip of the ridge at your two o'clock. Drop all weapons and surrender to the Gama Assault Commander immediately or I will *engage*. Over."

There was another click in my ear.

"Mic is cold," came from Command.

"Roger."

The ants stopped moving and turned to look up at me. Within a few seconds, Terran soldiers began to walk out of the base with their hands held high, some pointing up at me and my long shadow. They were greeted by a group of Gama soldiers who roughly pushed them around toward a waiting transport on the other side of the ridge. I heard cheering and it got louder by the second.

Below, the Gama troops were waving their guns and hands in the air as the chant of "Elite" could be heard over and over. The Terran soldiers continued to point my way and gesture to each other as they got shoved along.

"People will look at you like you're a god."

My father's words rang heavy in my head at that moment. I had just made fifty Terran soldiers surrender because I told them to.

Meanwhile, the Gamas' chant continued, and I looked up at the stars, trying to find where Palertine might be at that moment. To where my father would have been.

"You were right," I whispered up to him.

1

I sit outside now on a deck that leads into my office. With me sits a young man named Giovanni, whom Katrina and Jacqueline have hired to interview me and eventually write my biography. We both look out at a sea of green grass lined on two sides with tall, equally green trees. In the distance, my daughter's shiny silver ship, *Time Over Time*, sits, its three landing pads pressed into the soft grass. Between the ship and my home, I watch my wife, daughter, son-in-law, and three twenty-somethings play stickball. There is a great deal of verbal insults being thrown about along with an equal amount of laughter. It's a beautiful moment.

"Would you mind telling me what you're thinking right now, Mr. Ronin?" Giovanni interrupts said moment. I turn to him, taking a sip of two-hundred-year-old whiskey and carefully setting my glass down on my coaster so it's perfectly centered. It's strange to see all those wrinkles on my hand as I do that.

"Tell me, Giovanni," I answer, "most of my stories involve killing Terrans just like yourself. Will that bother you?"

Giovanni blinks at me for a second, taking a sip of his own drink.

"Well, as long as I'm not next on your list, I'm fine with it," he chuckles…nervously.

I smile a little inside, looking back out at the game in progress. I can feel Giovanni shuffling around a bit in his chair. Interestingly, in addition to the very high-grade recording device he has sitting on the glass table between us, he's taking notes with an ancient-style fountain pen and a simple pad of paper.

"Would you mind going back to sometime after your swing conversation with your father? Tell me about your training. What was it like? What did you do?"

Ah, yes. My early teenage years. A very mixed bag that time was.

2

I settle into my chair and begin telling Giovanni the early part of my tale.

"Training was training. You run. You jump. You exercise with weights and cardio. I fought with military instructors as well as other boys around my age that were also being groomed for high-level military work. There was book work and tests. Lots of studying of recent and ancient battles. Lots of strategy and planning. We were being molded day by day, week by week, and eventually year by year into the killing machines we would eventually become.

"At the time it was monotonous. I didn't hate it, though. In fact, I was very, *very* good at it. Top of my class in every subject. It was fun being the best. Fun to have the other boys look up to me and ask me how I managed to do things they couldn't. That part was fun. Other parts weren't.

"I never made any friends. I tried, but I always felt awkward. Every smile I seemed to find always shrank away into something else. Something that didn't like me or was intimidated by me or sometimes even afraid of me.

"That was my life, every day for four years. Wake up, breakfast with my mother and father, usually in silence, then class, then training, then home for homework. Eventually dinner and finally bedtime. I liked being alone in my room at night. I could pretend I was things I was not. I made up a lot of make-believe friends back then.

"When I was fourteen my father led me through a series of hallways in one of the buildings on the base. I thought nothing of it until he opened a door and we entered a room filled with high-ranking officers. In the middle of the room was a man tied to a chair, his arms twisted harshly behind him, and his mouth was taped over. The other side of the room stood two soldiers dressed in white plastic hazmat-style suits over their uniforms and mops and buckets next to them. I felt my heart begin to beat harder in my chest. My father walked me up to the tied-down man. He unholstered the pistol on his hip, cocked the hammer, and handed it to me.

"'Shoot him in the forehead,' he ordered, taking a step away.

"I stared at my father for a second, my hand beginning to shake. Then I looked over to the officers. I recognized one. His name was General Tony Montoya. He returned my gaze and spoke just as firmly as my father had.

"'Go on, Tanner. Do as your father told you.'

"I looked at this man in the chair. He was petrified. Tears streamed down his cheeks as his chest heaved up and down.

"'What did he do?' I asked my father, feeling more and more like the man in the chair as each second passed.

"'It doesn't matter, Tanner. He's Terran. Shoot him.'

"The man's eyes followed us back and forth. He looked at me, whining behind the tape over his mouth. Pleading with me. As hard as I tried, I couldn't stop the tears from flowing from my own eyes.

"'Father...I...I can't.' I did my own pleading. My father frowned and looked around the room. He stepped away quickly to a table, ripping something cloth off of it, and returned in the same quick steps. The cloth turned out to be a bag that he roughly pushed over the seated man's head. You could hear his muffled cries from inside.

"'Better?' My father glared at me.

"I don't know how many seconds went by. Two, five, ten? Maybe a hundred. It felt like hours standing in that room, feeling the eyes of important people burning into me. The unseen eyes of the man under the bag. My senses regressed to me hearing my own heart and seeing a now hidden face.

"However long it was, it was too long. My father ripped the pistol out of my hand, giving me a withering look of disappointment. He shot the seated man in the head with the same casualness you might toss a wad of paper into a bin. The two soldiers in the white hazmat suits immediately approached with their brooms and buckets to clean up the mess.

"My father took my hand in his and harshly pulled me toward the door.

"'Elite...' came from Montoya. My father whipped around to face him. I'd never seen him look so angry. He was practically frothing at the mouth. The two looked at each other for some time.

"I know!" my father hissed at the general, quickly finding some level of self-control. '...Sir.' He seemed to straighten, realizing the misstep. 'I *know, sir,* and I will handle it.'

Then I got dragged the rest of the way home. I was expecting to get beaten senseless, but he never laid a hand on me. However, what he did do was far worse. He stopped speaking to my mother and me. Utter silence in our household when he was home. We were too petrified of him to risk speaking to each other, so it was three months before anyone really spoke. I was back out on my swing, once again playing alone with my FollowMe ball.

"'Hello, Tanner,' he said with his stern, low voice.

"'Hello, Father,' I replied, suddenly feeling like that man in the chair.

"'You'll have to take that test again, you know.'

"No 'How are you?' No kind, parental greeting. Just straight to his point. I didn't say anything. I just stared down at the dirt and my shoes.

"'Next time you have to pull the trigger, boy. If you don't...' And he paused and I heard him take a deep breath.

"'Next time you *have* to," he finished, his voice turning dark and sinister. He stared down at me with heavy eyes for a long time. Eventually he got up from his swing and left.

"I called my FollowMe ball back and hugged it hard."

///

Giovanni looks at me, his eyes wider than they were a few minutes ago.

"That seems a bit…harsh, right?" he carefully asks.

I shrug in response.

"Did all the kids have to do that? The rest of your classmates?"

"I honestly don't know. If anyone else did, no one spoke of it. I never did. This is the first I've told that story to anyone. Even Katrina."

Giovanni writes furiously on his pad of paper for a moment.

"So, may I ask. Was there a second test?"

"Yes."

"And...what did you do?"

"I pulled the trigger."

Giovanni's eyebrows soar. He scribbles some more, then leans forward and checks his recording device. Seeming satisfied, he sits back.

"Can you elaborate? Why did you pull it the second time versus the first?"

I take another sip of whiskey. I have a feeling we're going to go through a lot of whiskey this evening.

"I was sixteen, so it helped I had another two years of training and just...*age*...under my belt. But mostly it was because I couldn't bear the thought of another three months...or worse...of silence from my father. My poor mother was a wreck during that time and I felt it was my fault. Still do really. But by the time I was sixteen I fully understood what I was going to become and what that entailed. So, I pulled the trigger and held it together until we got home. Then I went into my bathroom and vomited for an hour."

"What did your father say to you after you shot...excuse me...after you passed the test?"

"Not much. He took my mother and I out for a fancy dinner that night, if I recall. I remember a lot of toasts in my name and lots of slaps on my back and shoulders from mostly strangers. Officers that I had never met for the most part."

Giovanni looks visibly surprised.

"Really? No *attaboy*? Or an *I'm proud of you* or anything like that?"

I laugh loudly and refill my glass, handing the bottle over to Giovanni for him to do the same. He takes the bottle with a grunt, shaking his head.

"So, please, Mr. Ronin. Continue. What's next?"

What's next? Ah yes...

3

"Just before my eighteenth birthday our school received a new student. It was immediately apparent this young man was different from all of us. I've never had a homosexual thought or desire in my entire life, but I simply was in awe of how incredibly handsome this young man was. He was like some Old-Earth Greek god. Thin, chiseled angular face with a matching physique and a wickedly dark playful expression that both seemed to never change and also hide so much.

"Our instructor did the introductions in class, but at lunch on his first day he found me outside of our main training building, standing in a courtyard and reading new messages from my mother on my commcard. I was surrounded by lots of students not speaking to me.

"'I'm Canter,' he greeted, reaching his hand out to shake.

"'I'm Tanner. Tanner Ronin,' returning his shake. We had one of those brief testosterone-filled hand-squeezing contests that guys do.

"'I know.' He smiled a smile that I would become very familiar with over the coming years. 'I hear you're the shit around town. Mr. Future Elite Alpha himself.'

"'Well, I…I don't know about that,' I replied, strangely caught off-guard by this person.

"'Yeah, you're full of shit. You know exactly who you are. There's a problem with that, just so you know. I've gotta warn you ahead of time, seeing we're going to be best friends and such.'

"I blinked at this Canter person for a second, miles behind his train of thought.

"Best…friends?

"'Uh, what's that? What's the problem?'

"'Because I,' he said, smacking me hard on the shoulder, 'am going to be the Elite Alpha, and you're going to be my bitch, Elite Bravo!'

"'Thinking back now at that moment in time, Canter's words stirred something in me. The idea of me *not* becoming Elite Alpha someday had never even entered my mind. No one had ever challenged me. I was still the best of the best in my school and studies. Everything, really. So here now was this stranger that had me on my heels and talking to me in a way I had never been spoken to before. I remember my jaw mentally setting at the time.

"I don't think so...

"But my verbal response didn't come quick enough and Canter continued on, wildly changing the subject in a way I would never get used to.

"'Now, fancy pants, where the fuck do you get something edible around here? I'm starving.'

"'It's, uhh, this way. Mess hall. C'mon,' pointing across the courtyard. As we walked, I had to ask him something.

"'Do you really not have a last name?'

"He just laughed in response...and that was it. No answer. I harassed him about his name for years and years and always got the same response. It wasn't until a very long time later, after his passing, that I'd find out the truth."

4

"Canter...*Adams*," Giovanni confirms carefully. He looks like he's preemptively wincing.

"Yep. The one and only."

I pause, thinking of the man, and find myself adding in, "Literally," at the end of it. Giovanni taps away at his pad with his pen, appearing to try to figure out the next thing to say.

"What do you think of him now? After all that he did. To the Gama society. To you. To...Katrina?"

My blood briefly runs hot with the mention of Canter and Katrina in the same sentence. Not a bad question though, really. In the end, Canter fell victim to his own ego. His own obsession with a relationship with me that never existed. At least never on the level he thought it was.

"Canter was my best friend for a very long time," I finally answer, swirling the ice around in my glass and watching the liquid spin and dance for me. Giovanni sits silently, politely waiting for more.

The game in the yard has quieted and now many of the players have retreated to the house. I overhear murmurings of food and drink, so our kitchen is likely being raided. It's getting later in the afternoon and the shadows from the trees are growing quickly. Far off, Katrina and Jacqueline sit in the grass under one of the trees, chatting away. Jaxx pulls wads of grass up and tosses them absentmindedly to the side as Katrina makes fighter-jet motions with her hands as she speaks. The whole vision makes me smile inside. That said, I still have a hard time wrapping my head around the fact that my daughter now appears to be two decades older than her mother…

I turn back to Giovanni.

"He was the first person around my age to truly speak to me. To spend any amount of time with me. I had grown up without siblings, surrounded by children and then teenagers that were either intimidated by my family's name or just didn't like me. And then suddenly, one day, this amazingly charming young man comes out of nowhere and declares that we are now best friends. And that's exactly what happened. We became fast friends. We were inseparable."

Giovanni scribbles and speaks while looking down at his pad.

"What was he like? Were there red flags? Was he a…I mean…was he…*normal*…when you met him?"

Giovanni cringes at his own words.

"I'm sorry, I don't mean it like…" as his voice trails away.

I have to chuckle at that.

"Nothing about Canter was ever *normal*. I mean, it started with his name. And then his looks. I had only known him a couple of weeks when he proposed a double date after a conversation we had just finished."

"Conversation?" Giovanni's ears perk up.

Oh yes. *That* conversation…

5

"You're fucking kidding me." Canter looks at me like I have just confessed to murdering my family.

Fuck. I now regret my honesty. I want nothing more than to undo the last thirty seconds of my life.

I shrug.

"You're telling me that the one and only Tanner Ronin, the fucking heir to the Elite Alpha throne, number six in a line of Ronin Elites that span over two hundred years, at eighteen years of age has never been with a girl."

Another shrug. This sucks.

"You're a virgin." Canter doesn't ask a question, he states a fact.

Third shrug with a, "Yeah…" and a kick to the ground.

"Have you kissed a girl?" he pries.

I take a lengthy breath, the memories of pretty girls I know circling around in my head. Pretty girls I've only known at arm's length.

"No."

"Have you been on a fucking date, Tanner?" Canter yells, standing up from the park bench we were just sharing. His voice attracts the attention of a few fellow park dwellers. I motion for him to lower it, nervously looking about at the joggers and families milling about.

Canter's expression is more and more dumbfounded. I stand, embarrassed and frustrated at the same time.

"I don't know what to do," I growl at him, my teeth gritted with emotion. "I don't know what to say. No one ever taught me that. All I know is what I've been taught, and no one has taught me that shit. No one ever said, 'Here...do this and do that and say this and say that and a girl will like you.'"

Canter stares at me for a bit and then starts giggling.

Not cool.

"What the fuck, Canter?" which just makes him giggle more. He turns and puts an arm around my shoulder, squeezing me hard.

"I'm sorry, friend. It's just so ridiculous. You could have anyone you wanted, you realize that? Maybe you don't, but it's true. You're a half step away from being a god, Tanner. A fucking god. Soon, everyone you see here in this park will be worshiping all that you do."

That struck me.

"You sound like Father." I give him a slanted look as we walk.

He grins. "That's the nicest thing you've ever said to me."

6

Giovanni looks at me, his eyes full of curiosity.

"So?" he asks.

"So?" I ask back.

"Did he solve your…um…situation? You can't just leave it there."

I chuckle again.

"He did. He solved it in a very *Canter*-like way."

Giovanni leans in, readying his pen.

"Please do tell, Mr. Ronin."

I need another drink for this.

///

"Canter had an apartment. He had money and the means and no one to supervise him, so he chose to live off-base in the middle of the civilian world. Downtown Palertine. By comparison, the vast majority of the rest of us either lived with family in military-sponsored homes around the base or in the actual barracks on-base. Basically, as long as his grades were good and his training was approved, Canter could do whatever he wanted."

Giovanni is going mad with his note-taking.

"After *the* conversation, the next day Canter informed me that he had arranged a double date with two girls named Natashia and Catherine. Friends of his, as he described. And in addition, I needed to plan to stay overnight at his place downtown. I was somewhat stunned that my mother and father had no problem with this when I asked permission. On the contrary, they seemed enthusiastic about it. They didn't even ask why.

"So, we go out and Canter does all the talking. He's utterly charming to his core, saying all the right things to the girls, paying for everything, making them smile and laugh, just a complete fucking smooth operator on every level.

"Meanwhile, there's me, who has spoken all of four sentences to the opposite sex my entire life and all I can really manage is a nod here and an appropriately timed laugh there. But eventually we end up back at Canter's apartment. It was a very swanky and well-decorated place with all the best of everything and nothing out of place...which was weird for an eighteen-year-old boy. But anyway, Canter took 'his' date, Natashia, immediately back to his bedroom and Catherine and I were left on our own in his living room, sitting on a couch. It wasn't long before the sounds coming from the bedroom made it clear what was going on. Catherine took over, pulling my clothes off, and, with a hefty amount of coaching, was soon making similar sounds underneath me on the couch."

I catch a smirk on Giovanni's face with that statement, but he says nothing.

"I was entranced by this young woman. She was sweet to me. Kind and gentle and beautiful and obviously knew her way around things, so to speak. We lay next to each other on Canter's couch for a few minutes and I was thinking things like, 'Is this my girlfriend?' and 'Is this my future wife?' My mother's entire goal in life for me was to marry and start making grandchildren as soon as possible. I thought I had hit the proverbial ball out of the park on my first at-bat."

I stare at the floor now. This next part of the story is always a little tough.

"Canter's bedroom had grown quiet for a while when I heard him yell Catherine's name loudly. He demanded she come to his bedroom. To him. She looked at me and I felt a panic as I looked back at what was supposed to be the future mother of my children. The expression on her face was like I was a lost puppy. She gave a gentle caress on my cheek and stood, walking naked into Canter's bedroom. It wasn't long before I could hear her making the same sounds that she had just made with me."

Giovanni sits back in his seat, chewing on his pen.

"Shit," he says. I shrug, staring out at Katrina and Jacqueline still talking far away in our yard.

"That's a bit of a rough intro into things, right?" Giovanni continues.

"Well," I laugh a little, "that was Canter for you. *Technically*, his mission was a success. There were just some unfortunate casualties along the way. Namely me in that particular one. But that was his M.O. He was always successful with whatever was thrown his way, but never in the way you or I or most people would think. He had a surprising number of missions as an Elite where he needed to retrieve a secret Terran technology or weapon. Most of those missions he succeeded on the retrieval part, but for one reason or another the ships carrying the items back mysteriously disappeared or were destroyed."

"Were they ever found?"

"Of course," grinning, "always a bounty hunter or some pirate might send in an offer to sell with a high price. Sometimes we paid it. Sometimes we just flew out and killed them to take it. But they always circled around in one way or another. And Canter's bank account seemed to get bigger and bigger after each one of those missions. Not that I knew any of this at the time. This was all discovered years after his death. Although, it was highly suspected by much of the higher-ups."

"So he never got caught?" Giovanni asks, leaning back in his chair and taking a break from his paper pad.

"Not until he started doing all the stupid shit after Katrina showed up," motioning to my wife out in the grass.

Giovanni takes some notes and looks up.

"And then what?"

7

I sink back into my chair, the memories flowing over me. So many memories.

"That was our life for a while. We were the two top dogs in school, just a few short years away from becoming Elites. It turned out that Canter was right. The world was our oyster. We spent our days training and going to school and our nights with the most beautiful girls in the city. Canter seemed to have an almost unlimited supply of money and he spent it ravishingly on everyone around him, which was mostly me. This went on for a very long time.

"Eventually, we were sent on missions as part of our final training. Easy stuff. Safe stuff, just to get our feet wet. More than one time I was sniper support for my father. Those were my first *official* kills."

"What was it like to see your father in battle? To see him fight?" Giovanni asks.

I smile inside. I've never shared this with anyone. But…there is no reason for hiding anything at this point in my life.

"I wasn't impressed."

Giovanni looks surprised.

"Not impressed at watching Gama's…at the time…Greatest Warrior in combat?"

I shake my head, chuckling at Giovanni's response.

"Nope. That's the thing. I had a secret that to this day, only a few know about."

Giovanni tilts his head, eyeing me.

"Are you going to share?"

I refill my drink and offer the half-empty bottle to Giovanni, who takes it eagerly.

"When I was twenty, my father surprised me during my classes, excusing me from the classroom and instructor, very similar to when I was a young boy.

"I asked him what was going on, and he just smiled, congratulating me on my recent missions. We began to walk an eerily familiar walk."

"Like your tests?" Giovanni chirps, interrupting my train of thought.

I smile. And chew my lip a bit in annoyance.

"Yes. Exactly like my tests. And the end result was similar. A door opened to a room full of important people. Once again, there was General Montoya, standing stiff and straight with his traditional frown. However, much to my initial relief, there was no Terran tied to a chair in the middle of the room. No soldiers wearing hazmat suits. There was, however, Canter in attendance, which unnerved me a bit."

"Why? Why did you feel that way?" Giovanni interrupts again, and I give him a look. He swallows hard, shrinking a bit in his chair.

"I don't know. Clearly our relationship was…interesting…to put it conservatively. I found it odd that he was mixed in with generals and admirals and…my father. General Montoya spoke, telling me I was to fight my father one on one. Hand-to-hand combat."

Giovanni's eyebrows soar, but he stays quiet.

I find myself nodding to myself. *My secret*. I remember so vividly.

"The thing is, I guess my secret was that I had never given it my all. I never had to. I had never pushed myself to my own personal limit. And I was still the best. All those duels with my fellow students and our combat instructors and eventually, Canter himself. Maybe I had fought at eight-tenths. Once or twice at nine-tenths. But I had never pushed as hard as I could. And I knew the moment those words left Montoya's lips that my father had no chance against me."

"Really?" Giovanni murmurs quietly.

"Yes indeed."

The duel with my father plays in my head like it was moments ago. So clear. Every detail of every second burned in my memory like one lengthy slow-motion clip from a movie.

"It was quick, really. Over in a few seconds. My father and I, shirtless and facing each other in the middle of the room. The two of us surrounded on all sides by the VIPs. Canter was looking like he was about to burst in anticipation. My father lunged at me, going for an arm grab, and that's when I moved faster than I ever had before. I finally had an excuse to go my full ten-tenths. I might as well have teleported. So, I stepped aside and shoved him to the ground as if he were the slowest, weakest Terran to have ever walked. And then I backed away. There was this collective gasp in the room. My father...the look in his eyes...that *look*. I think *he knew* with just that one move. But he stood, brushing himself off, and came at me again. I picked him up with one arm and threw him into a crowd of officers with a force that put three of them in the hospital with broken bones."

I watch the pen fall out of Giovanni's hand.

"You *threw* your father. With one hand. I just want to make sure I got that right..."

"Correct," smiling at Giovanni's shocked expression.

"Everything went fairly crazy for a minute or so. People yelling and pointing and calling for medics. I remember glancing over to Canter and the look on his face is something I'll never forget as well. He knew at that moment that he would never best me. And that I had been toying with him all along. He may have been the champion of sociability and charm and master with the opposite sex, but he knew now that I was king of the battlefield. And he would never challenge that."

"What about your father?" Giovanni asked, genuinely riveted at this point.

"My father was fine. He got up and looked at me and gave me a nod. It was a gesture filled with things I still can't quite put a finger on. Anger. Frustration. But also, maybe some pride in there. Or that could have been hopeful thinking at the time.

"That would be the last time my father looked me in the eye. He may have been a crap father, but he was ever the professional soldier to the end. He tended his resignation as Elite Alpha to General Montoya on the spot."

"Shit…" Giovanni whispers.

"And that was that. Montoya promoted me to Elite Alpha seconds after my father resigned. My father congratulated me, shook my hand, gave me a pat on the shoulder, and left."

Giovanni stares off into space for a minute, tapping his pen on his lips. I genuinely wonder what he's thinking as I catch Jaxx and Katrina walking inside our home.

"Can we take a five-minute break? I just want to go over everything I've jotted down. This is amazing," he blurts out.

I smile. "See you in five," standing to go have a brief visit with my family inside.

8

"How's it going?" Kat smiles mischievously at me as I pile some cheese and dried meats on a paper plate in our kitchen. She knows this isn't something I wanted to do. She and Jaxx sort of forced it down my throat. I have to admit, Jaxx's pouting was the nail in the coffin for me.

"I want to know your story!" she demanded. She actually stomped her foot. Quite a sight to see a seventy-year-old woman stomping her foot at you.

"It's not that interesting," was my constant reply.

"OH MY GOD, DAD!"

Behind me, the rest of the middle-aged "children" and their own spawn have piled into our living room, searching for an Old-Earth movie to put on.

Looking back at Kat now, "Not bad actually. Been nice to talk about some things I haven't before."

She straightens, her eyes narrowing on mine.

"Never before?"

"Mmmhmmm," chewing. And grinning.

"Like, with *me*, never before?"

I turn around, grinning madly, and head back out to my office's deck. Katrina's voice is sharp behind me.

"You better fess up, mister!"

"You're next!" I yell over my shoulder as Giovanni exits a restroom to my left, smoothing his shirt, and nods, joining me in our brief journey to our interview arena.

9

"All right, sir. Now you're Elite Alpha. What's next?" Giovanni asks, shoving a massive amount of dried meat into his mouth. Katrina had dropped off a loaded plate for him seconds ago, giving me a scolding look as she left.

"More of the same, really. It was the Canter and Ronin show for a while. Fight by day and love by night. In the end, I enjoyed the fighting part a great deal more than the...loving part."

It goes quiet for a while. Giovanni scribbles, looks over his notes, checks his recorder, and finally breaks the silence.

"Is that when you eventually met Sandra? Did that change things?"

Sandra.

No. We're not there yet. Someone else before her would change everything.

"Not yet. Her name wasn't Sandra. Sandra was later. It was Mina."

I haven't spoken that name in decades. Many decades.

Giovanni doesn't speak, settling into his chair and looking expectantly at me. Our warm star is just finally setting, the darkness fully winning over the light as cool air now wraps herself around us all.

Mina.

"I need to preface this story with another," I say, taking a strong drink from my glass. Giovanni nods.

"Around two years after being made Elite Alpha, I had a younger Elite, Elite Lambda if I recall, named Xavier come into my office. He had just returned from a mission. He was timid and nervous and just acting like a wreck, which wasn't his normal self.

"After settling into the seat across from me, he finally began a confession about meeting two Terran soldiers during the battle he had returned from. Something about finding a blown-up transport and just trying to get some time to rest for a few minutes. He accidentally stumbled upon these two enemy soldiers, one male and the other female. Both assumed they were about to be slaughtered by him and they were understandably terrified, but Xavier had already had his fill that day and just wanted to sit still for a while. He ended up sitting down shoulder to shoulder with the female Terran. Her counterpart ran away, leaving her alone with Xavier. She was very unimpressed with her fellow Terran soldier's actions, as he described."

I laugh to myself at Xavier's words back then. He spoke perfect Terran and the insults he said she launched at the fleeing soldier were fantastic.

"Sir?" Giovanni asks, waiting for me.

Memories...

"Anyway...Xavier became more and more uncomfortable as he told this story. He knew everything was documented by helmet and body cams. But eventually he got to the point and said about the most surprising thing I'd heard in my life."

"Which was?"

"He told me he asked if he could kiss her."

"The female soldier!?" Giovanni blurts out.

"Yeah. Exactly. My same reaction at the time. So, I wait and eventually ask if he did or didn't and he finally says he ended up...well...kissing the girl."

Giovanni looks impressed, his bottom lip sticking out with a smirk.

"Now Xavier's problem here is that we have formal rules for interactions between Gama soldiers and enemy soldiers. It's pretty black and white. As long as you're killing the enemy, everything is copacetic. If you're doing anything *other* than trying to kill the enemy, that can be considered treason. So, theoretically, Xavier could be in serious trouble here. Now, that said, in the end, I'm Elite Alpha and I have the final say in cases like this with my Elites. And the truth is, I was genuinely more interested in his experience with this female Terran than concerned about protocol.

"So, I told him not to worry about anything. He was exceedingly grateful, shook my hand, and was leaving my office when I found myself unable to resist asking a simple question.

"'*Elite?*' I spoke sharply, knowing my tone would stop him in his tracks.

"'*Yes sir?*' Xavier paused at the doorway, turning to me and swallowing hard.

"'*Did she kiss you back?*'

"'He turned white as a sheet and he...he rubbed his face for a while like he was searching for something. He seemed to suddenly get quite emotional.

"*'Yes, sir, she did, sir.'*

"There was pain in his voice. Longing maybe. His last words to me were haunting.

"*'She's a special girl, sir. A very special girl,'* he said in a shaky whisper.

"And then he saluted and left."

I stop, looking at Giovanni as he looks back at me.

"That's it?" he asks.

"That's it."

"That's the *preface*?" he asks excitedly, shifting in his seat.

"Indeed, that's the preface. Here's the story for you," I chuckle in reply.

10

"You've got to be *fucking* kidding me," I grumble to Canter, looking over the wiring diagrams on my forearm tablet.

"You really should curse less, Tanner. It's unbecoming of you," Canter coyly replies, leaning against the gray-walled building we're supposed to be breaking into now.

"How can our intel be *this* bad?"

I hear Canter chuckle in my earpiece in response.

We should have been in and out of this place ten minutes ago. Actually…that's not right. We should have been out of here over an hour ago and in and out in ten minutes. I glance around at the huge, brown, granite mountains around us and the chaos in the valley below.

The first problem was location. How that was a problem, I can't even fathom. We've got a gazillion fancy instruments to tell us where we are and that still got fucked up. Second problem was the distraction, which consists of several hundred Terran and Gama grunts flogging away at each other in a valley about a mile south of where we are. Unfortunately, the battle, of which the only purpose was to support our mission, is about to literally die out. Basically, Canter and I are a few hours late and the two forces have killed each other to the point that there's not enough left to actually fight. Or... *distract*. And lastly, the wiring diagram we've been given to hack into the rear door of this place is entirely wrong. Completely wrong. Everything is just a cluster-fuck.

"Do you like Amy or Jamie's tits more?" Canter asks, jarring me away from my frustrations. I look and his Elite mask is staring up at the darkening sky in thought.

"Canter, we have a *task* and we have a *timeline*. Focus."

"Task and timeline?" he laughs. "So avant-garde of you, Mr. Elite Alpha."

As I look back down to study the diagrams on my tablet more, *it* happens.

"Excuse me?" spoken in a high-pitched Terran voice from just yards away.

And with those two words, everything in my life changes. Everything.

Somehow, amid Canter's and my bickering, a single female Terran soldier has snuck up on us. The two greatest Gama warriors have been duped by a simple grunt. I turn to see a diminutive figure lit up by the two bright moons above, her arms raised and her saggy BDUs far too large for her frame, walking slowly our way.

///

"Now," I pause my story, sitting up and leaning in toward Giovanni, "I have to tell you that I am a student of Elite history. You need to understand that every single Elite mission, going back to our origins, seven hundred years ago, has been documented in some form. Maybe it was body cameras or microphones or drones or a military camera crew, whatever. Point is *everything* is and has been documented. I myself have reviewed and studied *thousands* of hours of footage. And there are scholars out there, many of them, who have reviewed and written endless papers and theses about these recordings. And I can tell you that without a doubt, in the seven-hundred-year history of Elites, not one single Terran soldier has ever *voluntarily* walked up to one of us. Not one. Not ever."

I'm poking my finger in the air at Giovanni to make my point and I can tell the tone of my voice is a little too...*passionate*. His eyes have grown wide and he's paused his note-taking as he simply nods in reply to my rant.

Leaning back in my chair, I continue.

///

Canter's reaction is instant and pure *Elite.* With one swift move he's pulled his rifle off his back, aimed, and fired. The entire movement takes less than half a second.

Had I not been his peer, the young woman's head would have vanished into a mist of blood and brains, but I managed to barely knock the tip of his rifle barrel with the back of my hand so his shot sailed just over her hair.

She ducks, far too late for it to have made a difference, but doesn't stop her cautious, wobbly advance on the rocky ground under her.

"Please don't kill me," she repeats several times as I feel Canter slowly turn to look at me. I can sense the expression of rage behind his mask.

"I want to know what she wants," I reply to his unasked question. He stares at me and I can feel his expression change to a combination of irritation and complete disbelief.

"Time and task, Tanner. Time and task," his voice sarcastically hisses in my earpiece. He turns and takes over working on the lock.

I pull my rifle off my back and take a few steps toward this young woman who has absolutely blown my mind.

11

"That's close enough," I say to her, pointing my rifle at her chest.

"Please don't shoot. I'm not armed. I come in peace," she replies, her voice wavering and her hands still held high in the air.

"Is there something wrong with you? Are you ill?" I ask.

It's the only thing that makes any sense to me. Is it possible she's simply lost her mind? I glance around, looking beyond her for signs this might be some kind of Terran trap.

"Can you pass along a message for me? That's all I want. That's why I walked up here."

A cold wind that started earlier has increased. At some point in her journey to our position she's ditched her helmet so her dark hair is getting blown around her face. Distractingly, I find her quite pretty.

"Who came with you?"

"No one. I was sniping. I got bored and started looking around with my scope and caught you two up here. That's it."

Shit. We're dumbasses. I curse Canter's and my own insouciance. But what did she say...?

A message?

"Did you say, a *message*?" I confirm. My Terran is good but not perfect.

"Yes."

"To whom?" utterly dumfounded.

"To one of you. To an Elite. I met him two months ago in a battle on Churix Six."

...Holy...shit...

It's her.

This is the girl that Xavier talked about. That was the battle he had just returned from. I drop my rifle to my side and take the few remaining steps up to her. I can feel a kind of strange excitement in me. Something I've never felt before. I rerun the entire conversation between myself and Xavier in my head.

"Put your hands down," I order and she does, looking up at me. I tap the side of my helmet, raising my mask so I can speak directly with her.

She seems a little startled at my face being exposed but her eyes quickly narrow on mine. My stomach tightens a bit at her reaction to me. She makes me nervous.

"Did you...*converse*...with an Elite Marine?" deciding to change the question slightly at the last second.

She swallows, her eyes darting about in some level of shyness. In the end, she looks up at me and nods.

"Yes, sir."

"And that's who the message is for? The one you...*conversed*...with?"

"Yes, sir."

"What's the message?"

She shuffles around for a second, suddenly at a loss for words. Eventually she looks back up.

"I guess, just that I hope he's okay and that I think of him. A lot. You know. Something like that."

"*Something like that?*" I ask in disbelief.

"Yes, sir. Please..."

"You walk all the way from there," pointing over her shoulder to the battle over a mile away, "and up to two Elites that you know will likely just blow your head off, and that's it? That's all you've got? '*Something like that*'?"

She shrugs, nervously wringing her hands.

"I'm a soldier sir, not so much a poet or anything like that."

"Are you insane?" I blurt out, something inside of me utterly confused with her. She actually smiles at my question, grinning up at me.

"If you asked my family, I am. My daddy especially. He thinks I'm just crazy as anything most of the time."

I laugh at her response.

I laughed...?

And in that moment, I have a realization. *She just made me laugh.* All those evenings and nights with Canter's girls, not one ever made me laugh. Not one single one.

"Sir?" the girl interrupts my thoughts. "You asked if I had talked to him. Does that mean you know him?" she asks.

"I do," I reply and her reaction is amazing. Her eyes light up and go wide as she claps her hands together.

"You *know* him?!"

"Yes."

"And he told you what happened?"

"He did."

"And did he say anything about me? Maybe something…more?" The sheer amount of hope in her eyes tugs at my heart.

Canter's irritated voice slices into the moment.

"I'm in. Now get rid of your pet and let's go, Elite," his voice hisses into my earpiece.

"Sir?" the girl pushes.

"Hang on." I put my hand up.

"Right behind you," I reply to Canter, glancing his way.

I'm in a strange place now. Technically, I should be executing this girl. However, I don't think I could live with myself if I did that. I could let her go, but now that's a risk of treason…even for me. I vividly remember Xavier's pained words from weeks ago.

"She's a very special girl."

Indeed, she appears to be just that.

A completely terrible idea forms in my head. A series of bad decisions, but it seems the best option for all parties involved. I guess all parties excluding me. And Canter.

Oye.

"Do you want to see him?" I ask the girl.

Now she looks at me like I'm the crazy one.

"...What?"

"Do you want to see the Elite that you kissed?" looking her in the eye. Hers go wide and she blinks at me.

"I...I mean, yes, but, how?"

"I can take you to him. You'll have to come with me now. To my Gama home planet. I can promise your safety but not much more."

Tanner...what are you doing here?

The girl pauses, thinking. She looks back over her shoulder to the battleground in the distance. We both watch as transports silently land and take off, looking like really cool toys from this far away.

"You need to decide right now," I push, knowing I've got an angry Canter to deal with in the building.

"Will I ever be able to go back to my home?" she asks.

"I don't know," is my honest reply.

"If I want to leave now will you kill me?"

"No." I shake my head, filling myself with regrets.

She thinks again, rubbing her face with her hands in a way remarkably similar to Xavier's actions while in my office.

"I'm leaving," I say.

"I'll come with you!" she yelps, reaching for and grabbing my left arm. I pause, looking down at her. Her touch sends sensations through me that I've never felt before. It's like hot electricity running under my skin.

"I want to see him," she says, her eyes filled with determination and something else I've never seen before. But whatever it is, it's magic.

"Come," motioning her to follow me. The two of us head into the building.

12

The past two and a half hours have been about the most entertaining I've had in my life.

The young soldier's name is Mina Hunter and she is now sitting on my knee, well into our hyper-jump back home. Around us, sitting and standing, are eight Gama soldiers who know just enough Terran to be entirely entertained by this young woman's hilarious stories of her childhood. The fact that little Mina knows a bit of Gama herself has helped.

In the back of the transport, Canter sulks, furious at the fact that I'd bring a Terran onto the transport with us.

"A fucking monkey!?" he screamed at me when I found him in the building with Mina at my side.

"Have you lost your mind, Tanner?" he raged.

But I kept her safe from him, as I promised, and now she's the center of attention on our ship.

Something else to irritate Canter, who's normally the one doing the storytelling.

"Tell it again!" a Gama officer asks, grinning like a ten-year-old boy.

"Tell what?" Mina replies, grinning back.

"The one where you tried to fly off your roof!" he roars and the rest of the group enthusiastically agree, clapping their hands and slapping their thighs.

"Well, if you insist." Mina glances at me with eyes that make my chest feel strange and starts the story once again.

I see it. I see what Xavier saw in this girl. She's nothing like any person I've met, and I'm pretty sure nothing like any of my fellow Gama soldiers have met.

Eventually, much to the chagrin of everyone except Canter, we land. I quietly motion for the soldiers to listen and I tell them something that comes from the heart.

"Next time you go and buy some poor Terran girl from the Dog Cages, remember her," nodding at Mina.

Their expressions universally change, the smiles sliding away into thoughtfulness, and I get a number of "Sirs" and nods in response. They all say their farewells to Mina in a wistful, sad kind of way.

Canter is long gone and Mina has her hand in the crook of my arm as we walk down the ramp from the transport to the landing pad, hundreds of feet above the city below at the top of a skyscraper. I ring Xavier using my Elite suit.

"Elite Alpha, sir?" he answers.

"Are you home?" I ask.

"Yes, sir."

"Good. I'll be there in a couple minutes. I have a surprise for you."

"Uh...yes, sir. I am not really..."

I hang up just to mess with him a bit.

Mina and I walk to an elevator, confounding a group of civilian Gamas waiting to take their own transport. I'm sure none have seen an Elite arm-in-arm with a Terran in their respective military attire.

Less than a minute later the two of us are standing at the door of Xavier's apartment. Mina is so nervous she's shaking. I stare down at her in continued amazement.

"What's more frightening? Walking up to two Elites on a battlefield or waiting now?" I ask, pointing at the door.

"Waiting. Definitely waiting." She chews furiously on her lip. I shake my head and ring his doorbell.

"Shit shit shit," Mina curses quietly in Terran.

Said door is ripped open before she finishes her cursing and Xavier's eyes immediately lock onto Mina.

Silence, quickly followed by disbelief, quickly followed by electricity flows between the two of them. I watch in total fascination.

"You..." Xavier stammers in Terran, his eyes dancing all over her.

"Hi. Hello. I hope this is okay." That look of hopefulness Mina had a few hours ago on a faraway planet has returned with a vengeance. Her eyes never leave his. They just blink away as she gazes up at him.

Xavier looks at me, his eyes wide and mouth hanging open in raw confusion and surprise.

"What's...what's this? What is...?"

I take a step away, feeling...*knowing*...I'm the intruder in this moment.

"We'll figure it all out. Don't worry," trying to become invisible.

And then the two *really* look at each other. I see that extra something I saw earlier in her eyes as clear as day in both of theirs now. There's a connection...an energy...between the two that is awe-inspiring. Both hesitantly reach for each other and then quickly fall into a fierce embrace.

I have officially worn out my welcome.

"Elite," I nod, saluting Xavier. I step away, heading down the hall.

"Sir!" I hear him call out from behind me.

Turning, I see Mina pressing herself into him and tears streaming down Xavier's cheeks. A mix of a thrill and a chill run all through me.

"Yes?"

"Thank you, sir. I don't understand, but thank you."

"We'll talk tomorrow, Elite. Have a good night."

I find the elevator, smiling for the two and, I have to say, envious of Xavier right now. That look they shared. That moment. I know now that that is what I want in my life. I want to find someone who looks at me in that way and look the same back at her. I have heard of it spoke of off and on from others. Never in my own family but mostly from Old-Earth movies and books I've read. It's a simple word I never appreciated until this moment.

Love.

They call it...love.

That's what I want.

13

Giovanni stares at me with a fair amount of confusion on his face.

"What's the problem?" I ask, reading his expression.

He thinks, his eyes moving around briefly.

"It's just…not…I mean…it's not what I was expecting."

"Expecting?"

"I guess I came here to listen to endless tales of battles and adventures and you conquering and killing…everything. But you've told me a story about essentially the opposite of all that." Giovanni chews thoughtfully on his pen after saying this.

"Not enough action for you?" I smile, settling further into my seat. The night has fully won the evening and Giovanni and I now sit under the dim lights from my office and the moons above.

I can faintly hear the whispers from my family inside watching their movie.

He chuckles at my response, shaking his head.

"No...it's just that I'm going to have to tell the publisher they are not getting the story I was sent here for."

I smile more and shrug a bit, reaching for my glass again.

"So, what happened to Xavier and Mina? It sounds like a match made in heaven, unfortunately for you, right?" Giovanni leans back, relaxing and looking more and more comfortable with the interview by the second. I think the drinks have helped quite a bit.

I think back to Mina. She was so beautiful and so charming. The two of them so madly in love with each other.

"Xavier and Mina were very happy together. Because of who I was, my role and rank as Elite Alpha, I got two or three invites per week to join them on their nights out. I selfishly accepted most of those invites, if anything to spend a little time with Mina. Things went swimmingly for four weeks until I got a call from Xavier. A terrible call."

"Terrible?" Giovanni asks, his head tilting.

I think back...remembering dark moments. Very dark moments indeed.

14

Xavier's number is buzzing on my commcard as I walk to the grocery store near my building and I answer, expecting the next invitation. I'd be lying if I wasn't a little excited to see it.

"Elite?"

"Elite...Tanner...I need help." Xavier's voice is high-pitched and shaky and filled with terrible things.

"Xavier?" I stop in my tracks, standing straight. Something about his tone sends goosebumps up and down my back.

"She's gone, sir. Someone killed her. Someone killed my Mina."

The world spins as Xavier's impossible words sink into me. To my left I glimpse a park bench and sink into it, my skin feeling wet and clammy.

"What, Xavier? What has happened?"

"I just got home from a mission, sir. She's in our bed. Her neck is broken. She's gone, sir." There is a sob in that last part.

"I'll be right there," I reply, hanging up. But I can't quite get up. My legs and body don't seem to work in this moment. I have to pause and take some breaths, running my hands over my thighs and knees to try to recover. My skin is cold and sticky, and I feel nauseous as I try to process what I've just been told. Xavier's apartment is less than five minutes away and eventually I find something inside of me that allows me to stumble there with great haste.

15

The civilian and military police know who I am and let me past the computerized yellow tape into Xavier's apartment with a mix of nods, salutes, and bows.

Xavier himself is sitting in a chair in his living room, his forehead in his palms, staring at the floor. I immediately locate the chief investigator by his uniform and approach him. Beyond, in Xavier's bedroom, I can see a dimly lit figure in the bed. The shape of Mina, surrounded by detectives and forensic investigators, carefully probing around her, makes me ill.

"Cameras?" I begin with the investigator. He looks at me nervously.

"Elite Alpha, sir," replying, "Nothing. The cameras were disabled."

I take this as the apartment's cameras were disabled.

"What about the others? Hallway? Elevator? Entrance?" I ask impatiently, turning away from the figure in the bedroom, trying not to see it...trying not to see *her*. The image screams in my head.

"Everything, sir. The building was disabled. All of it."

I look at the investigator, his words sinking in.

Impossible.

The thought that I am one of the few creatures on this or any near star system capable of something like that runs through me. That only someone with my level of training...an Elite...would be capable of executing something like that...

For the second time today, a chill...a very deep chill...runs through me.

"Everything?" I look down to the investigator, confirming.

"Yes sir, everything."

"Any prints? Fingers? Shoes? Gloves? Anything?"

"Nothing yet, sir," he replies, swallowing hard as he looks up at me.

"DNA?" I hiss.

He shakes his head, as a bead of sweat forms on his temple.

Fuck.

Fuck fuck fuck.

I know who to talk to. I know who did this.

I walk to Xavier and give him a squeeze on his shoulder.

"You have someone coming?" I ask, doing my best to keep my voice steady.

"Yes sir. My sister and aunt are on their way," he manages, his eyes a wreck from tears.

Another shoulder squeeze and I'm gone. Gone to confront Mina's murderer.

16

I ignore the "call" button next to his door and give it a good hard rap with my knuckles. A lengthy rap at that, anger...no, *fury*...fueling my intrusion. I can vaguely hear movement inside before it opens.

"Tanner?" he asks, looking surprised to see me. At least I think that's surprise on his face.

"Why did you do it?" I growl, pushing... forcing...my way into his home. He steps back, his hand on his chest.

"Tanner, what are you talking about? What's wrong, my friend?" His head tilts in a funny way that I don't like.

"Canter," I'm shaking, "why did you do...*it*?"

There is a pause and he looks me up and down.

"Would you like a drink, Tanner? You seem like you need a drink," he says, moving away from me, into his small kitchen. My eyes rake across the familiar landscape of his apartment where

I've spent so very many evenings and nights with him and his...guests.

That said, I don't reply, I just stare at him, stalking to where he is, as he pours two drinks.

"Tanner, you really need to take a breath and tell me what's going on. You're not yourself right now," he says with a very controlled amount of concern in his voice.

I find my voice again.

"Why, Canter?"

"Why...what?" He hands me my drink. I take it and turn, sitting down on the white couch I've spent far too much time on. I'm a mess of pain and anger and hate and...much more. For a moment I stare at my shaking hand and then down at the drink and stare off into space.

I vaguely hear Canter's voice behind me, calling my name. I hear a lot of noise as I stare into nothingness. It's just lost in the storm that's my head now. That said, the voice...*his voice*...grows louder. Much louder and much more angry. Maybe it was my lack of response, I'm not sure, but he eventually digresses to primal shrieks. Turns out he's screaming at me at the top of his lungs.

It takes a second or more to absorb, but eventually Canter's last words sink in. Like something slowly pulled into a black tar pit, never to escape.

"She was a distraction!" in a high-pitched voice.

She was a distraction.

That pulls me out of the abyss I'm in and I stand, turning to him as sweat drips from his face.

"A distraction?"

Canters eyes are wide in a very not-normal way.

"Are you kidding me, Tanner? What is your problem? You're upset over that little monkey girl? She's nothing!"

His eyes grow wider as he clenches his teeth. He looks like a kind of twisted cartoon character.

"Xavier and you are idiots for fawning over some Terran whore the way you did. Show some Gama pride for the love of God!"

I've had enough.

I rush him, grabbing Canter by his armpits and lifting and shoving him against the wall a few feet behind. He's a feather in my grasp and his eyes betray that he feels that. I see fear. A first in our lengthy relationship. It fuels the fire inside of me.

"She was a good person, Canter. She was...*wonderful*. She was beautiful and sweet and kind. You had no right to do what you did." It's my turn to scream, squeezing my fingers and causing him to wince and writhe in pain.

"Let me go, Tanner. You've lost your mind," he growls back.

I toss him down to the ground and watch both my hands shake violently from adrenaline.

Canter is on his feet instantly.

Elite.

But not me. Not *Elite Alpha.*

He feels the danger he could be in right now.

"This is how you treat me? Really?" he hisses, spittle flying from his mouth.

"Are you not happy with what we have, Tanner? Our time together? Our nights out with each other and...*my* friends? Don't you enjoy them? Is that not enough? What makes you think you *deserve* my attention? My friends' attention? You know it's me that's the reason they put up with your fumbling. What makes you think you can replace our time together with some stupid Terran monkey?"

He glares at me, panting and looking like a madman as I try to process the ramblings. Somehow, someway, his words find something deep in me and I pause, suddenly feeling small again.

"Get the fuck out of my home, Tanner. Get the fuck away from me. You've clearly lost your way and possibly your mind. We are done, you understand? You and I are finished because of a worthless Terran ape. Remember that. Remember what you have lost because of that."

He points over my shoulder to the front door of the apartment.

"Get the fuck out!"

I'm done now. I have no energy to fight, mentally or physically. I stare at this person in front of me for a while. This person who has been my best and only friend and I wonder where he went. It's easy for me to turn away and just walk out of his home. Minutes later, it's far more painful to open the door to my own home knowing that my life is without Mina in it.

17

Giovanni is leaning back and looking at me. You can see the wheels spinning in his head.

"So…what happened to Canter?"

"Nothing." I shrug. His eyebrows soar.

"What? He murdered a girl. The girlfriend of an Elite, no less."

If only…

"He murdered a Terran slave. A worthless POW. You're talking about a military culture that organized the process of capturing and selling Terrans for the recreational pleasure of its soldiers. She was nothing."

Giovanni stares at me, dumbfounded.

"But there had to be hell to pay when Xavier found out, right? What did he do?"

Oh boy.

"I couldn't risk some internal strife in my Elite ranks. No way I could have that. We had known about a Terran spy that was living a few floors below Xavier for nearly a year. We had been quietly watching him, monitoring him day and night. I spent a few evenings at home editing and splicing a series of security camera videos together that made it look like he was the murderer. I presented it to both Xavier and the chief investigator. Being Elite Alpha at the time, my word was golden and the Terran was quietly handed over to Xavier."

"Jesus…" Giovanni whispers.

"So, I kept any drama away from my Elites, Canter stayed clean, Xavier had his revenge, and the police investigator was happy. Win win win all around," I say, sighing a little as I finish.

"Except Mina was gone." Giovanni reads my mind.

"Bingo."

18

Silence. Or near silence, minus the rustling breeze through the trees. I stare into nothingness, remembering that sweet young woman.

"Do you want to stop? It's dark now," Giovanni offers.

"Do you?" I reply, enjoying the moist cool air I'm breathing in.

"Not really. I'm good if you are."

"I'm good. What's next?"

Giovanni shuffles through his notes, his eyebrows furrowing. Katrina briefly leans around my office door, winking and blowing a kiss. I smile and nod, returning her affection from a distance. She's gone before Giovanni finally looks up.

"Would you mind telling me about Sandra?" he asks, shifting nervously in his seat.

As he should.

That's a subject to tread lightly around. My ex-lover and Jackson's mother...

No. Sandra is not going to be a part of this.

"Sandra was a spectacular person. Fiery and beautiful. But I'm not sure there's much to discuss. I captured her during a battle, essentially giving her the choice to die or live with me. She chose the latter. I had hoped that she might be my Mina, but she never loved me. We quickly became roommates and after a year and a half, I helped arrange for her to live on her own in Palertine. As you know, she eventually fell in love with my good friend Vince Daniels and they had a son, Jack, who's now my son-in-law."

Giovanni looks disappointed. He stares at me, his pen not moving for one of the few times in the evening.

"Nothing more?"

"Nothing more, I'm afraid."

"All right," he sighs as he starts flipping around in his notepad again.

I think of the Sandra that was my girlfriend and lover for a few brief months and those memories pale in comparison to memories of her as Katrina's best friend and my own friend's wife. It's so strange to think we had that relationship together so long ago.

"Just," I look up at Giovanni, "make sure your words are kind when speaking about her. Whatever other research you've done on your own, she was a very special person."

Giovanni nods.

"And," I feel I have to add, "I'm very proud of what Jack did to avenge his mother and father's death. And I was honored to have been a part of it."

Giovanni pauses, nodding again, already knowing that part of the story. Everyone does.

19

"What about Elite Daniels?" Giovanni asks quietly.

"Vince?"

"Yes. When did you meet? May I ask?"

"We met after Canter went away. After Mina. Canter just up and vanished for nearly two years after our fight. I needed a Number One. A potential new Elite Bravo and a young Elite around my age was transferred into Palertine from a distant Gama star system."

"Was it similar to Canter in how you two got along?"

I have to laugh at that. Loudly.

"Absolutely lot," taking a drink. "Vince was quiet and was somewhat socially awkward. He had no friends, coming from so far away. Very similar to me, to be honest. But the first time I stood with him on a battlefield, I knew this was my man. My next Bravo. He was a god on the battlefield."

"Finally," Giovanni chuckles back at me, "a mention of a battle."

I raise my glass sarcastically back at him.

"And that's really it. Very simple. We grew to be good friends, but nothing like Canter and I had been. It wasn't until Katrina showed up and he eventually met Sandra that things got closer between us. And then, of course, Canter and the Farohs took me away for twenty Palertine years, so that put a damper on our friendship."

"Of course." Giovanni smiles, shrugging a little in sympathy.

"That's it?" he confirms.

"Honestly, that's it. He was a great man. A gentleman and a hero. I think of and miss him every day."

"All right, then the next one may rub you the wrong way. Let me know if I've stepped over a boundary." He looks me in the eye and I smirk back at him.

"Fire away, Terran."

I think the drinks have finally started to catch up with me.

20

"With all due respect, Mr. Ronin, I must ask about your age. You appear *at least* twice as old as Mrs. Ronin. How are your feelings about that?" Giovanni asks carefully, his eyes showing their hesitation.

I smile inside. Another secret.

"I suppose you should ask Katrina, right?" smirking and doing a terrible job of hiding my inner glee.

"I'm not interviewing Mrs. Ronin right now, sir."

Ah...suddenly Mr. Formality.

For a few seconds I'm torn between hiding what has been hidden for decades or selfishly enjoying telling a little story.

Screw it.

"Turn your recorder off. In fact, give to me," I say to him, my voice dropping low.

"Sir?" He straightens in his seat.

"This is off the record. You can hear but you cannot tell, understood?"

He blinks at me, and his expression changes to frustration.

"But sir, for the book. Your story. If it's something of…"

"You decide, Giovanni. It's black or white. And if I trust you, then know I'll *find you,* if you break that trust. Understood?"

I say the words "find you" very slowly.

He sits back as if pushed by my reply. I watch his chest start to move up and down more quickly.

"Do you want to know?" I push, keeping my eyes on his.

We stare at each other for several seconds until he finally relents and leans forward, switching off his recorder. He sits back and waits.

"Paper and pad." I motion to the table between us with my eyes.

He frowns, but obliges, setting his beloved note-taking tools down. I stop and take both a lengthy breath and a drink before continuing. He's locked on me the entire time.

"You are aware I have two grandchildren, correct?"

"Yes sir."

"Did you not notice a third young man playing out in the yard this evening with the others?"

"I did, sir."

"And did you not wonder who that was?"

Giovanni shifts in his seat, his eyes narrowing on me.

"Not at all, sir. I assumed a friend or neighbor. Nothing more. I didn't think one moment about it."

Ah, how to draw this out…even for another few seconds.

"You can't ponder a guess, maybe?" I smile at him.

He looks around, thinking for a quick bit before looking back at me, curiosity killing him.

"I can't, sir. Should I know?"

"No, you should not," I reply, reaching over and filling his drink. I sit back and just look at him, overjoyed at the tension that's been built.

"Sir?"

"C'mon, just a guess? Give it a go, for Christ sakes."

Now he looks bewildered, looking around the roof of my deck, waving his drink about.

"I'm sorry, sir. I...dunno...Jack has a secret brother or something like that?"

I cannot torture him any longer.

"He's Maximillian Adams."

Giovanni freezes, staring at me with big eyes. It takes quite some time before he responds.

"Sir?"

I just nod to reaffirm what I've said.

"I—" He looks for his words, pointing first out into the yard and then behind me into the house. "Adams? Admiral Adams?"

"One and the same."

He downs his drink. I laugh a bit as I lean over for the second time in a couple minutes to refill it. His eyes are as wide as they've been this evening as he looks at me.

"I'm sorry, but I don't understand, sir. I mean...that's not...I mean Admiral Adams died three years ago. He was over a hundred years old." He frowns.

"It's why Katrina appears so young. Adams figured out some very big stuff decades ago. He brought Katrina back from the dead, mostly with a considerable amount of luck. Skipping the details, he spent the time between then and his own passing to minimize the *luck* part of things. So, he's still with us, just now as a nineteen-year-old young man."

As I look over to Giovanni, I feel I may have broken him. I wait for him to respond and it takes quite a while.

"Katrina died? Wait..." he finally manages, closing his eyes and shaking his head.

"She did."

"DIED?"

"Yes, *died*. Buried in the ground dead. And Adams brought her back to life nine months later."

"But she was captured by Gamas. In prison for a while. The funeral was fake. Some kind of military distraction or something. That's what's documented. That's what's official," gesturing madly at me.

"It's bullshit."

"Sir!"

"Bullshit."

"Are you serious?"

"I am. And are you connecting the dots? Do you see how I'm answering your question?"

"You're going to do the same?"

Giovanni's gone pale.

"Exactly," smiling at him.

"And, Katrina thinks this is…?"

"It's her call. When she's tired of this old man," motioning at myself, "I have a thirty-five-year-old version of 'me' waiting. It's a little more complicated than that, but you get the idea."

He stares at me, disbelief written all over his face.

"You see, many years ago, my daughter and son-in-law taught my wife and I something.

Katrina and I always knew we were meant for each other, but Jack and Jacqueline told us it was more than just that. We were special. We were what are called Swans in some parts of the galaxy. Inseparable, even by death. Kat and I both agreed that death itself would not be a factor in us being together...or not. That *we* would decide when things would end, if it ever did. And we have Adams to thank for that."

Giovanni stares at me and swigs his drink again.

"I need a break," he mumbles, getting up. A little more wobbly this time around.

I laugh.

"Are we done?" I ask.

"No!" he answers, his arm reaching for the doorway. "Not yet. A couple more questions for tonight."

He stops and looks back.

"Katrina really died?"

I laugh, sort of. *Ugh*. Terrible memories.

"Yes, yes, she did, unfortunately."

"And Adams also?"

"Yes…well, sort of. His was on purpose. If that makes any sense."

Giovanni blinks at that response.

"And he's out there tonight, you know, running around and stuff? Like, younger than me?"

"Yes."

"And you're not messing with me? No bullshit?"

"No."

"…Holy shit," he murmurs, running his fingers through his hair as he disappears into the house.

21

Giovanni has settled back into his seat as music has now joined our night ambience. Someone inside has turned on some Old-Earth classics and they croon softly in the background as my interviewer looks around for the source.

"They love Old-Earth music," I offer. We have a fresh bottle of Scotch on the table between us and he takes a lengthy breath before starting.

"Two more questions for this evening," he says, almost apologetically.

"Have at it," I reply, filling both our glasses.

"I must have a battle. Tell me of your greatest, please, sir."

I've been to more planets and star systems than I can remember. I have no idea how many battles I've fought in nor the number of species I've fought against. But I will say, I do have a number one here. A top battle that changed everything...again...for me. And I had no idea at the time.

"Yes, I have it," I start. Giovanni visibly sighs in relief, readying his pen and glancing to make sure his recorder is on.

Just as I begin to tell my tale, Katrina silently rises up behind his seat. Her face and eyes highlighted by orange moons, I worry for a moment for his welfare. I've seen that look before...on our missions. It's never been a good thing for those she's gazed upon.

But once she stands, folding her arms across her, her lethal eyes soften into something far more welcoming. She holds a finger up to her lips, shushing me, blessing me with a hint of a smile. I smirk, and look down to the coffee table separating my interviewer and myself, making sure I don't give away the position of my Number One.

I collect myself and start my story.

"It was a strange battle, really. A large one, settled deep into a canyon of a rocky planet on the fringe of the Durian star system. We had what should have been a relatively unimportant base that the Terrans threw several hundred soldiers at for reasons none of us could comprehend. But, yes, it was big. Very big. Four or five hundred to a side. The battlefield, mostly just black vulcanized rock and red clay, was set in darkness when things progressed. It was a mayhem of firepower and infantry hand-to-hand attacks. I spent most of the battle up on a hillside, watching and sniping on occasion. The ground was lit by a mix of our weaponry and the three small moons above, which gave everything a bluish tint.

"The Terrans had advanced from my right to left to where they were at the doorstep of the base at the point of the canyon. Directly in front of me lay a trench we had built to redirect some seasonal flooding, and many of the Terran soldiers had hunkered down into that trench.

"Then I got a call in my helmet.

"'Elite Alpha. Status Mission Priority Zero. Eliminate the transport on sector fiver-seven-fiver. You have fifteen seconds.'"

Giovanni pauses, furrowing his brow at me.

"Fifteen seconds?"

I interrupt my own story…again…eager to elaborate and welcoming his reaction.

"Bingo. My thoughts exactly at the time. But it's worse than that. The 'Status' in 'Status Mission' means that the success or failure of my efforts will directly affect my rank as an Elite. And the 'Priority Zero' part is unheard of. Our priorities are normally five through one. One being the highest and very, very rare. Zeros are Unicorns. I've done hundreds, maybe even thousands of missions and only three were Priority Zero, and this was the first. I knew then that if I failed with a mission of this level, I was done as Elite Alpha. The icing on the cake was that between myself and this transport, I had about a hundred yards of armed-to-the-teeth Terrans and another hundred yards of space after them to run to transport."

"In fifteen seconds…" he wheezes.

"Yeah. In fifteen seconds," stealing a quick glance up at Kat. She's backed away from Giovanni's chair a bit, hiding herself in the shadows of the deck, but I can see just her cheek bone and lips in the moonlight. She's gorgeous and it both warms my old heart and gives me chills at the same time.

My Elite. My girl.

"So?" He refocuses me, and I catch those moonlit lips smirk.

"Right. I spent a second or two very pissed off, grabbing my rifle off my back and seeing all of three rounds remaining. I realized that wasn't going to work, plus I had no heavy weapons to shoot the damn thing down with, so I pulled out my blades, turned my Elite eyes up as bright as they would go and dove into the mass of Terrans in front of me."

Giovanni blinks.

"The first part wasn't too bad. They tried to get away from me. They tried their best to get out of my way. They were terrified. But the second half, they just piled into each other. It was a wall of soldiers I had to…*cut*…my way through. Those last few yards were…*difficult*."

I shiver now, thinking of those terrible moments. So many lives fell in those seconds under the edges of my blades. One particular thing hits me.

"You know," looking out into the night sky, "this may be something you want to keep out of your book, but, in my time as an Elite, I had felt the sensation of my blades going through fabric and armor and flesh and bone, but this night was the first I had felt the sensation of cutting through teeth. It was not a good sensation."

He curses softly.

"You made it through, then?"

I nod, taking a strong drink from my glass. Kat's face has emerged from the shadows and I see some tears on her cheeks. It's everything I have to stay seated and not to rush to her.

"I did. I had about five seconds left. I could see the transport starting to take off. The landing gear springing up as the weight it had to bear was lightened and the blue jets pushing it away from the ground. I ran as fast as I could, which, I have to say, was very fast."

I smile a bit at that part. I was ungodly fast, once upon a time.

"I had two grenades on me and my goal was to have not one but two miracle throws into the landing gear bays with a hope that would do the trick. At the time I gave myself a one-in-five chance I'd make the throws. But then, as the transport rose into the air, the pilot made an unbelievable mistake and spun the thing around one-eighty, presenting a closing hatch to me just a few yards away. What was a near impossible throw turned into something I could have underhanded the grenades into from a mile away. I stopped running...I remember my feet sliding on the cement...and tossed both grenades easily into the hatch. It finished closing and a second later, the transport blew into a million pieces, showering me and everything nearby with melted metal and fire."

"You succeeded!" Giovanni says excitedly. He looks like he may applaud.

"Very much so."

"And then?"

"Well, behind me were about three hundred very angry Terrans. They all decided to shoot at me."

"Oh shit."

"Once again, you've managed to perfectly summarize my thoughts at the time. I ran. And I was fine in the end. But that success was enough to cement my status as Elite Alpha. It defined my career and changed my life in a way I had no idea at the time."

I have to purposefully not look at Kat again.

"What do you mean?" he asks, sipping on his drink. I watch as my Elite steps out of the shadows.

"It was the first time I saw him," she says quietly, her eyes locked onto mine.

22

Giovanni's reaction is spectacular. He yelps like I've stuck him with an electric prod, tossing both his pad and pen high into the air.

Kat and I both instinctively switch to our Elite reflexes. I watch her eyes grow wide as she locks onto the pen soaring in front of her, spinning slowly in the air.

The pad has bounced off the railing near me and I reach my hand out, waiting for it to arrive in my grasp. His yelp has been transformed into a low-pitched, lengthy "Arrgh." Kat and I have time to smile at each other as we catch our respective writing tools before things return to normal.

"How long have you been there!" Giovanni leans back, twisting and looking over his shoulder at Katrina. She hands him his pen and steps around his wide chair and sits down, joining him. I set his pad of paper down on the table between us.

"A few minutes. I wanted to hear Tanner tell his version of that story. He's never shared it with me."

"Oh..." he resets, gathering his pad and adjusting both his glasses and the pen in his hand. Katrina gives me a mock scolding look but it warms immediately, causing my old heart to flutter.

"You—" Giovanni stumbles on his words a bit, looking warily at her. "You said it was the first time you saw him. You mean Elite Ronin?"

"Yes. Exactly," she answers, her eyes still on mine.

"What did you see?" he asks, fully recovered.

"I saw a terrible thing," Katrina answers, her voice still very quiet, and now her eyes leave me.

"I watched a creature with the devil's eyes mow through my fellow soldiers like they...were...were made of paper. I was in that trench that Tanner spoke of. Just feet away from this monster that passed by me in a blur while bodies were shredded and tossed in every direction. Hands and pieces of faces and all sorts of body parts came raining down next to where I was sitting. And blood. Just...so much blood. And then, after all that, there was the explosion of the transport and the monster's figure in silhouette lit by the fireball. It was surreal and terrifying and...helpless. I had seen Elites before on the battlefield. But not like this. Not like him."

Katrina shudders and returns her gaze to me, pressing, pushing me into my seat. My heart fills with strange mix of guilt and love. She continues.

"So, that was how I first saw Tanner. He was a monster with glowing eyes and I went to sleep that night and had my first nightmare of that monster. I'd dream of him killing me every night for two years. The last memory of those nightmares always being that terrible Elite mask looking down upon me. It wasn't until I met him and understood what he really was that the dreams stopped. Even after that, it took a while before the dreams...the bad dreams...fully ceased."

Her eyes change to hold an apology as we look across the short distance of the table to each other. Giovanni is scribbling away, looking back and forth between the two of us.

"MOM!" comes loudly from inside the house. Katrina smiles and stands, walking to me and kissing me softly on my head.

"My monster," she whispers in my ear.

"Yours always," I whisper back, chills running down my neck and spine. It's been decades, but I'm still dumbfounded she is mine.

I get another kiss and she turns, disappearing into our home.

Giovanni watches this in silence. He understands. He gets it. I like him more now than any time in the previous two hours or so.

"If I may, sir. I have an idea of what I want to call your story."

"Yes?"

"I want to keep it very simple. Just one word. To the point, if you get my drift."

"...Yes?"

He swallows at my tone and begins to speak but I interrupt him.

"Have you thought about interviewing Katrina?" I ask, filling both our drinks again for the hundredth time tonight.

He pauses.

"I…I would be very interested in that, sir. But I haven't spoken of anything along those lines. I'm here to interview you."

"Can you stay a few days? Three or four? Enough to sit down with her and get the whole story? Her story."

Giovanni seems more and more surprised by this conversation.

"I do, sir. I have time. I only reserved a hotel for one night as I expected to be heading home after we finished tomorrow."

I wave my hand at him, dismissing his comment.

"You can stay here. God knows we have plenty of space," pointing inside.

He looks back and forth between me and the interior of my home.

"So?" I push.

"I mean…do you think that your wife will want to be interviewed?" Giovanni asks a valid question.

I know Kat enough that it will take some convincing and a couple of drinks, but she'll eventually sing like a bird once things get rolling.

"I assure you she will tell you a hell of a tale," I reassure him.

He sits up, visibly processing this new information.

"So?" I push again.

"Well, yes sir, that would be amazing. Yes. Thank you. I have to say I am without the…umm…most of the basics, if you know what I mean. I didn't even bring a toothbrush."

"We'll sort that out. This house is a revolving door of guests, so don't worry," chuckling a bit.

It's silent for an awkward bit as I feel Giovanni and I both figuring out what to say next.

"Can you tell me about the first time you met Katrina, sir?" he asks hesitantly, his eyes following her unseen figure inside of the house.

I can't hide a smile.

Oh yes…returning to a distant past. I close my eyes, remembering…

23

I'm having a damn fine day.

This is a hell of a thought at this moment, considering in the past nine hours I've been captured by the enemy, spit and urinated on by the guards, tortured twice by all means of electrical devices, and now strung up on a wall in a dingy, smelly, damp prison cell with my hands held high over my head in tight binds.

Fantastic fucking day. Maybe the best ever.

I'm smiling despite all this as I stare at the cold cement between my boots. I smile because just fifteen or so feet away sits the most amazing creature I've ever met in my entire life.

A few hours ago she walked in as part of the second round of torture. Armed to the teeth and dressed in oversized body armor, she put a spell on me the moment she entered the tiny interrogation room. The important thing here is, *I know I cast a similar spell on her.*

We stole glances at each other while I was being tortured. Honestly, I don't even recall feeling any pain, I was so mesmerized by this young woman.

When they were done I looked up and she was horrified. Almost in tears as she looked down on my messy, sweaty figure that was bound so tightly to the interrogation chair. When they untied me and dragged me to my feet I made sure I gave her a wink as I passed by, just to let her know I was all right. Just to show that I felt the same something in me that I think she was feeling in her. Her eyes did something in response that I didn't really understand, but it felt good. Really good.

And now, a few hours later and we're together again. Alone. Except for the obnoxious Gama soldiers nearby that have just recently fallen asleep.

It's been more dancing of glances. Me to her and her to me. Occasionally our eyes actually catch each other and it's like a switch is flipped. It's just like watching Xavier and Mina together that first moment they stood face to face at Xavier's door.

But this time it's me. Not someone I know. I'm the one that has been given the gift of that gaze. This girl is looking at me.

Lost in my thoughts for a moment, I am surprised to suddenly see the toes of Terran boots on the floor in front of my own boot. I look up and there she is...inches away.

Dear Mother of God...

She is stunning. Unreal. All sorts of fancy words I'm not smart enough to use. But she's right in front of me looking every bit how I feel. The veins on her neck pulsing away as drops of sweat form and slide down her forehead and temple.

She looks at me for a very long moment before her eyes leave mine and glance up at my restraints. I hear the snap of a clasp and watch as she pulls her pistol out of its holster and very slowly places it against my own temple. She pushes the barrel firmly against my head before leaning in and...

No way.

....Kissing me.

Really kissing me. I've kissed a few girls in my time, but this is another level. Her energy and passion and that extra something that's been going back and forth between us…it's all there in one singular, wet, slow, surreal kiss.

Far too soon she stops and starts to pull away. All I want to do is grab her and pull everything she is to me, to gently crush her figure to mine and hold her for the rest of my life.

But I can't, feeling my fingers high above gripping nothing in frantic frustration. So, my only option to keep her with me is to bite her departing lower lip. Not hard. Just enough to keep her with me.

Her reaction is…well, it's simply indescribable.

She presses her beautiful body into mine, a soft, almost silent, moan coming from somewhere deep inside as I feel a singular, powerful tremor against me. It's sexy and sensuous and like her eyes, filled with so much more.

Unfortunately, she quickly finds her feet and I feel her pistol push into my temple. There's still a soldier in there, whatever this moment we're having, so I release her lip and she steps away, breathing hard…just like me.

Her expression is exactly how I feel and we stare at each other again for a lengthy amount of time before her replacement quietly arrives and surprises the shit out of both of us.

What a moment.

///

I look back up to Giovanni, returning to the cool evening on my deck.

"As she left, she turned and gave me one last look for the night. That was it. That was the moment I knew she was my everything."

"Holy shit." He shakes his head at me.

"What she didn't know was the next guard was a Gama spy and released me. I ended up turning off the prison's forcefield, allowing it to be easily taken over by my Gama forces. We blew the crap out of the place.

"But more than anything, I knew I had to track down that girl. I knew I had to find her. Every bit of my life depended on finding that amazing young woman. Every single ounce of it. And I eventually did a couple days later."

Giovanni raises his glass.

"Well done."

"Indeed." I raise my glass back.

"And that's it," I say before taking a drink.

He pauses.

"Sir?"

"That's it. The end."

"That's it? I don't…"

"Yes. That's it. That's my story."

He stares at me for a second before…

"Wait…sir?"

"That's my story. Everything after that is Katrina's. I stopped being a 'me' in that moment and my life became an 'our' or 'we' or however you say it."

Giovanni looks horrified.

"Are you serious, sir?"

"Completely."

You would have thought I'd kicked him in the stomach, so I tried to be the nice guy for once and reach out with a question.

"What was it about the title or something you mentioned earlier?" I ask.

He blinks at me, recovering.

"I…um…yes, sir. Like I mentioned, I just wanted to keep it simple."

He's very flustered, blinking away and looking around as he thinks.

"All right?" I say, still attempting to be "nice."

"So, I'm thinking, just call it *Elite*."

Elite.

My own story with the title of *Elite* on it. At first it sounds like it's a good fit. I think of sexy ebook covers with my younger face splayed across them and *Elite* at the top.

But those thoughts are quickly replaced by those of Katrina. I think of what she's come from and what she's accomplished. I think of her speed and her skill and her sometimes bitter ruthlessness. She is the fastest there has ever been and on top of all that, she is still considered Gama's greatest fighter pilot. I think that in the next few days Kat will tell Giovanni a story far more worthy of a title as simple but perfect as *Elite*. That's what she is. She is and always will be the best of us.

"No." I shake my head, smiling at my own thoughts. "No, that won't do for me. Think of something else. Save that title for Katrina's story."

Giovanni nods, stopping and thinking about something for a while. I listen to the murmurs inside my home as he ponders whatever he's pondering. Quite some time, many minutes, go by in silence as he and I go to our own places for a while. I focus on the laughter I can just hear inside and the cool, moist air here on the deck.

Eventually he clears his throat and sits up. He puts his pad and paper down and then turns his recorder off, leaning forward rather formally in his seat.

"May I ask you one more question, sir? Just between you and I?"

"Certainly," intrigued at his actions.

He squints, thinking and chewing on his lip. If I were to guess, it seems like he's getting a little emotional. He finally takes a great big breath and speaks.

"I lost my father when I was sixteen, sir. An accident. I, umm, I have to say that he and I had a relationship similar to how you describe yourself and your father's relationship."

He pauses again and I watch the muscles in his jaw flex.

"I was curious, did you ever…were you ever able to reconcile with him? I know he passed just a few years ago."

Oh my.

He finishes off another drink and watches me, waiting.

Another set of memories washes over me. Very different from the ones we have been discussing tonight.

"Let me go get something from my office."

"Of course," he replies.

I stand, a little wobbly from tonight's libations, and walk the few feet from the deck into my office, circling around my desk. It's dark, but the moons and memory provide just enough to navigate. On the very right side of the top of the desk sits a four-inch-by-four-inch clear plastic square encasing a piece of paper. I pick it up and return to my seat outside, all the while brushing my fingers over the face of the square. I stare at the words on the paper as I start speaking to Giovanni.

"I was here when I got the message that my father was in critical condition. I wasn't going to go see him, but Katrina insisted. My mother had already passed the previous year and I did not go then and Kat was ruthless with her scolding. This time she was even more so. I grudgingly agreed to her demands and we took our ship, which is as fast as anything in the galaxy. The Denauge star system is very, very far away from here. A third of the galaxy. The trip took many days and, despite our great speed, he had passed by the time we arrived.

"The doctors and nurses that cared for him were very kind. They shared stories of his last days and hours. Ever the ornery son of a bitch, he was an Elite to the end. Cursing away at the illness that was winning over him in his final battle."

It's my turn to take a deep breath and it suddenly seems extra silent. Even the wildlife around my home is apparently listening in on the story.

"After all the formalities, the nurses took me aside and gave me a napkin. Unable to speak and shaking like a leaf, my father had tirelessly pointed at one just hours before he passed. The nurses eventually figured it out and gave him what he asked for. He wrote two words on it and then, through some lengthy hand gestures, instructed the nurses to give the napkin to me when I arrived."

"He knew you were on your way?" Giovanni asks quietly.

"He did," I reply and lean over, handing the plastic case to him. He takes it and exhales sharply through pursed lips as he reads the words. Again, the muscles in his jaw move and it's clear that he appreciates what those words represent.

Two words. Two very simple words written in very shaky handwriting with blue ink.

good son

Giovanni looks up at me, swallowing hard. I speak before he can say anything.

"I was seventy-seven years old when my father passed away. That's the first and only time he ever called me 'son.'"

He seems to get it, nodding and I watch a single tear run down his cheek as he leans over and hands the case back to me. He clears his throat.

"I'm happy for you, sir."

"Thank you," taking the case and looking at the handwriting for the thousandth time. I clear my own throat.

"I'm sorry that you lost your father," I offer.

"Yeah..." His voice cracks a bit and I feel I need to end this evening before things get more...well...I need to end this night. I'm tired.

"So, that's it. Get inside and tell Katrina the plan for her own story." I motion toward the door into my office.

"Yes, sir." Giovanni starts gathering his things as I look out at the darkness of my front lawn.

I can feel him looking at me and I turn. He wants to say something, but I'm well and truly done with talking this evening.

"Get going before you become the NEXT Terran on my list, got it?" I growl at him and quickly stand, towering over his figure.

For a moment I see what I have seen in so many Terrans' eyes.

Fear.

Genuine, pure fear of me and all that I represent. All that I am. All that I've trained to be and all that I have succeeded at.

Fear.

And then I wink at him.

"Go," I say again, smiling a little and nodding at the doorway.

"Sir...I..." he replies, a cautious smile forming.

"Now!" pointing.

His smile grows a little more before he rushes into the house, stumbling into my office and out of sight.

"Thank you, sir!" I hear from inside my office.

Finished.

I walk over to the railing of the deck and grip it in my hands, leaning over and looking up at the stars.

I think of the look on Giovanni's face just seconds ago as well as the words of my father from a distant past. I imagine my father looking down at me from somewhere up there in the stars, and before I know it, it seems like another figure joins him.

Vince...

"I've still got it," winking up at them.

I've still got it...

The End

Thank you so very much for spending time with Tanner and the Elite series. For more information, please visit johnmarktucker.com for updates and details on up-coming books. If you have a moment to leave a kind word or two on Amazon, that would be magic!

Again, thanks so much and there is much more in the future.

All the best to you and yours,

John

Made in the USA
San Bernardino, CA
19 January 2019